HARLEY HITCH

TAKES FLIGHT

HARLEY HITCH

TAKES FLIGHT

VASHTI HARDY

ILLUSTRATED BY
GEORGE ERMOS

■SCHOLASTIC

Published in the UK by Scholastic, 2024
1 London Bridge, London, SE1 9BG
Scholastic Ireland, 89E Lagan Road,
Dublin Industrial Estate, Glasnevin, Dublin, D11 HP5F

SCHOLASTIC and associated logos are trademarks
and/or registered trademarks of Scholastic Inc.

Text © Vashti Hardy, 2024
Illustrations © George Ermos, 2024

The right of Vashti Hardy and George Ermos to be identified
as the author and illustrator of this work has been asserted by them
under the Copyright, Designs and Patents Act 1988.

ISBN 978 0702 32344 7

A CIP catalogue record for this book
is available from the British Library.

Printed in Great Britain by Clays Ltd, Elcograf S.p.A.
Paper made from wood grown in sustainable forests
and other controlled sources.

1 3 5 7 9 10 8 6 4 2

This is a work of fiction. Names, characters, places, incidents
and dialogues are products of the author's imagination or are used
fictitiously. Any resemblance to actual people, living or dead,
events or locales is entirely coincidental.

www.scholastic.co.uk

For Romy –
be uniquely you and
always dream big and bright

CHAPTER 1

SUMMER

Not a cloud filled the sky above Forgetown on the first day of the summer holidays.

Harley burst like exploding popcorn from the front door of Hitch House before pausing to take an enormous breath, arms and legs stretched like a starfish, fingertips tickling the breeze, and bare toes scrunching the grass. "Welcome, SUMMER!"

Her best friend, Cosmo, strolled up the path

towards her and shook his head with a grin. "You're so dramatic, Harley."

"Well, you're under-dramatic, so I have to compensate!" She gave him a friendly nudge. "Can't you smell it, though?"

"Smell what?"

"Flowers, ice cream, strawberries, sunshine ... the bees buzzing."

Cosmo nudged Harley back. "You can't smell that!"

She winked at him. "Oh, can't I?"

Sprocket, Harley's robot pet, chased a butterfly along Grandpa Eden's flower-filled border. His eyes shone with hearts.

Harley jumped after him, catching him in a hug. "*He* loves the summer holidays, don't you, pooch? We get to spend all day together."

Sprocket let out a happy robotic bark.

"I can't believe Professor Fretshaw won't let us bring our robot pets to school," she said. "Loads of robots are there already, like the garden-bots and Primbot the gatekeeper... Hey, maybe we should petition in the autumn!"

"Hmm, we could, I suppose," Cosmo murmured.

Harley knew Cosmo well and didn't need to look up to know his shoulders had slumped. "Gosh. I'm sorry, Cosmo. Sometimes I forget you haven't got a pet." She jumped up as though her next thought was a spring inside her. "Maybe you could get one this summer! You've been in Forgetown practically a whole year now, and I know your mum didn't want you to have one at first, but surely now—"

"Harley, stop before you get all overexcited. Every time I try to talk to Mum about it, she says she's too busy with work to discuss it. She keeps saying 'maybe later'."

"Perfect!"

He frowned. "Did you hear a word I just said?"

She nodded emphatically. "Later follows now, and as now has been happening while we speak, it must be later already, right now, this very minute, so it's a *perfect* time to ask her again!" Harley's mind was already buzzing with what sort of robot pet Cosmo could get. Perhaps another dog like Sprocket, then they could be friends too, or a cat might be fun, or maybe something that loved plants as much as Cosmo did, like a robot butterfly?

"Let's go and ask her on the way to the Iron Forest! You can get all sorts of basic robot kits these days, and we can see what's growing in the Iron Forest and start thinking about adaptations. Sprocket loves getting upgrades, don't you, boy?"

"Much as I admire your waterfall of optimism, my house isn't on the way to the forest, and it would be a complete waste of time anyway. Mum said she's going to be tied up all summer with a hugely important town project. She's already spoken to your grandpas to make sure it's OK for me to spend more time at your house. She told me I could only interrupt her with life-or-death problems."

"This *is* life or death!" said Harley.

He raised his eyebrows doubtfully.

"All right, it's not, but it is really, really, really, really, really important."

"What's really important?" Grandpa Elliot emerged from the house carrying a picnic basket. He wore neat tweed trousers, a shirt and waistcoat, ready for work at the newspaper, with his chain digi-watch tucked in his pocket. He smiled a hello through his bright white beard, and his eyebrows pinched in curiosity.

"We were just saying that Cosmo should get a robot pet!" Harley told him.

"That would be nice. What does Mrs Willoughby think?"

"My mum says she's too busy to be fussed about pets," said Cosmo.

"Then that's your answer, I'm afraid," said

7

Grandpa Elliot. "But don't worry, Cosmo – you're like one of the family. You can come and play with Sprocket any time, can't he, Harley?"

Sprocket yipped in agreement and licked Cosmo's hand with his metal tongue.

"Of course." Harley liked to find ways round things, but it seemed that getting Cosmo his own robot pet wasn't going to happen yet. She let out a disappointed sigh. "So, what's the big project your mum's working on?"

Cosmo shrugged. "She said I'll find out soon enough. Oh, but she did say she needs to talk to you, Mr Hitch."

"How curious," said Grandpa Elliot. "It's probably some sort of official town business. They like to put notices in the newspapers for such things."

"Maybe it's a new shop! Or they're extending the star-chatter observatory?" Harley knew Professor

Orbit wanted a new telescope and a space education centre.

Grandpa Elliot passed Harley the picnic basket. "Time will tell. Anyway, what are you two planning to do in the Iron Forest today?"

"Summer holidays aren't for planning, Grandpa Elliot. We'll probably set up camp, do some foraging and add some adaptations to Sprocket."

"That sounds fun."

"Did someone say fun?" Grandpa Eden called from the greenhouse door.

Daisy the mechani-weather-bot trundled out ahead of him, clasping a bowl of strawberries, each one as large as a peach.

"Wow, Grandpa Eden, that's the biggest crop yet!" said Harley, licking her lips.

In contrast to Grandpa Elliot, Grandpa Eden was always a little messy in appearance with his summer shirt and shorts dusted with soil, gardening tools, seeds and gloves stuffed in his pockets, and his peppery-grey hair and beard, which were both usually in need of a trim. "Indeed. The super-grow feed has delivered in both size and number. It seems I hit the formula just right this year. It was a little too powerful during the autumn of the slug."

Cosmo shivered. "Don't remind me."

The previous year, Harley had accidentally super-sized a slug in the greenhouse to the size of a seal. She shrugged. "Slugsy wasn't a bad pet in the end."

The slug had eventually returned to its normal size and been released back into the wild, but Harley had quite liked looking after him.

"I see the fruit worked well for the natural hair dye too," said Grandpa Eden.

Harley gave a twirl. "I love my summer hair! It's like strawberry ice cream."

"The strawberries, cherries, camellia, roses and a dash of pomegranate were just the thing." Grandpa Eden nodded, satisfied.

"Maybe we could colour Cosmo's hair too?" Harley teased her hand through his dark curls, inspecting them curiously, wondering if the dye would take.

Cosmo drew away, aghast. "Er, much as I like the colour you've gone for, my mum would likely blow a gasket, maybe two."

"But it's the holidays, so it's not like you'd have to go to *school* with pink hair. We can be summer twins and surprise her!"

"Er, Harley," said Grandpa Elliot, "it would be absolutely necessary to get Mrs Willoughby's permission for anything like that, as you well know."

"I know." She smiled. "I was only kidding, although it *would* be fun."

Cosmo took a step back from Harley. "I'm entirely happy enjoying your hair experiments from a distance."

"Very wise," said Grandpa Elliot. "Harley and Eden dyed my beard once for a charity event at the newspaper. They promised it would come out in one wash, yet I was left with a lime-green moustache for three months! It clashed terribly with my waistcoats."

Grandpa Eden took the large bowl of strawberries from Daisy and passed it to Cosmo. "Here, take these to the Iron Forest too. Leave any berries you don't eat for the wildlife. The insects, especially ironstings, love a good strawberry. Ironstings are important to the ecosystem of the Iron Forest."

"Thanks, Grandpas," said Harley.

Sprocket dropped Harley's trainers in front of her. She wriggled her feet inside, then grabbed

Cosmo's wrist and tugged him along the path.

"Have a nice day, both of you!" called Grandpa Eden.

"Call on your digi-watch if you need us!" added Grandpa Elliot.

"We will!" Harley replied, although she knew they wouldn't need to. It was just a picnic in the forest. What could go wrong?

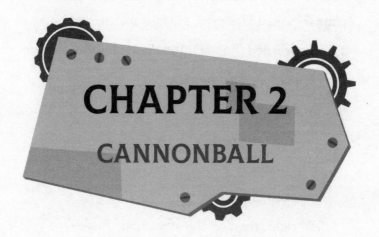

CHAPTER 2
CANNONBALL

The two friends jogged into the Iron Forest, laughing and chatting about all the ways they might adapt Sprocket, while the robot dog pranced at their heels.

"Maybe we could use a branch of the umbrella palm to make some sort of flying contraption for him, like a parachute? Or wings!"

"You mean the *Chamaerops umbraculo cogo ver*?" said Cosmo.

"Do you know all the fancy names for the plants?" asked Harley.

"I've learned the scientific names for those in the Iron Forest," he said proudly.

"Needle pine?"

"*Pinus ferrumacus.*"

"Silver oak?"

"*Quercus argentum.*"

"All right, then … the steel many-blade?"

"*Cordyline ferro multis laminis.*"

"Impressive."

Plants were Cosmo's favourite thing, whereas Harley loved the stars and the sky most of all; she spent many of her free hours at the star-chatter observatory. She adored the Iron Forest too, but Cosmo was the only person she knew who was as fascinated by plants as much as Grandpa Eden. She thought back proudly to the previous autumn when

Cosmo had saved the Iron Forest from a dangerous fungus by brewing a special formula and painting it on the fungus to get rid of it.

"The Iron Forest grows all sorts this time of year," she said. "It was August when Grandpa Eden found his wheelbarrow growing on an iron oak tree. Professor Horatio says the forest's unique iron-bio-thingy makes anything possible."

"*Thingy* isn't a scientific term."

"I'll have you know that *thingy* works for just about any ... thingy. For example: pass me the thingy, or what's that thingy on your head?"

Cosmo flinched and spun as though an insect had landed in his hair.

"That was an *example*, Mr Worry-pants."

"I knew that."

"Here, this spot is perfect! There's a bit of sun and loads of interesting plants around, *and* we're not far from the rusty willows and the lake so we might see a velocipede, or some ironhogs!"

They set up camp in the shade of a pretty, golden hazel tree and started to forage in the surrounding ferns for nuts, bolts and anything unusual. In the first hour they'd collected some brass cogs, wire weed and a few small light bulbs sprouting at the base of a cogweed plant. Harley jumped with excitement when she found them and had the brainwave that they could be turned into some sort of disco mechanism for Sprocket!

By ten o'clock, Harley insisted it was lunchtime because "summer has no rules", and they laid out their picnic blanket in the dappled sunshine and stuffed themselves with cheese sandwiches, scones, jam, cream, strawberries and home-made lemonade.

"This is the life," Harley said, sighing. "Maybe we should cancel autumn and stay in summer forever."

"But then the leaves wouldn't fall and there would be all sorts of tree diseases spreading."

"Oh, stop being so practical!" Then she sighed. "But perhaps you're right. If it *were* summer all the time I'd just want to lie in the sun and eat ice cream all day." She sat up. "We need to liven up. How about a game of powerball?"

Sprocket, who had been lying on his back beside Harley, warming his belly, flipped over with an enthusiastic *yip*.

"But powerball with a *difference*," she continued. "Instead of catching with our hands, we'll use a bat!"

"Did you bring one?"

"No need." Harley looked around and found a sturdy branch that had fallen from an iron oak. "This is perfect!"

"Don't swing it near me!"

"You go wide and field, and I'll bat. Sprocket,

set to full power. I'm feeling lucky…" She gripped her makeshift bat and set her focus. She'd played powerball with Sprocket all her life and her aim was near perfect. "Go!"

The ball shot into the air and she hit it hard with a *pop* that echoed around the forest, sending birds flying. Her problem on this occasion, though, was that she hadn't considered what she was aiming for. The ball flew like a cannonball, then thwacked into something bulbous hanging from a tree a short distance away. The ball dropped to the ground as the object I had struck swung from side to side overhead.

Cosmo ran a few steps, then skidded to a halt as he looked up. "What did you hit?"

Harley squinted as a strange vibration rustled the leaves above. A bad feeling made the hairs on her arm stand up. "Oh dear…"

"Don't say *oh dear*, Harley. Things never turn out well when you say that."

She screwed up her nose. "I *think* I hit an ironsting nest."

Cosmo didn't even have time to roll his eyes before angry buzzing erupted.

Grabbing his wrist, Harley yelled, "RUN!"

Abandoning their camp, Harley and Cosmo bolted for the edge of the Iron Forest.

"Ironstings won't leave the boundary of the forest. Come on!" Harley urged Cosmo onward as she leaped over cogweed and narrowly missed a patch of oil pods. The swarm of ironstings thrummed furiously behind them. "We're nearly there!"

Sprocket, who thought it was all some great game, twisted between Harley and Cosmo's legs. Harley was used to him doing that, but as they reached the edge of the forest, Cosmo tripped

as Sprocket zigzagged in front. Cosmo launched forward into the sunlight beyond the forest before landing sprawled on the ground in front of Harley. Thankfully, the buzz from the ironstings had faded.

"We made it! That was close." She reached a hand to help Cosmo up, but he didn't move.

"Ow!"

"Are you hurt?" asked Harley.

"I think one stung me."

She grabbed Cosmo under the armpits from behind and pulled him up, then spun him round and scanned his arms and legs for a mark. "Let me see."

"Not likely!" he protested.

"Why ever not?"

"Because it stung me … *behind*."

"Behind where?" She frowned as Cosmo turned beetroot red. Then it dawned on her. "Oh! It got you on the actual *behind*." She winced. "That's going to hurt. Grandpa Eden said he was stung there as a boy and it burned hotter than a Scotch bonnet chilli."

Cosmo's eyes watered. "You're not helping!"

"Sorry. We should get you to Dr Charm's apothecary in town. She'll have an ointment or something to help. We can get our stuff later. The ironstings will hopefully have eaten all our strawberries and forgiven us by then."

CHAPTER 3
ICE CREAM AND IDEAS

After Cosmo had seen Dr Charm and been given a plaster, he felt a lot better, and Harley promised him an ice cream to cheer him up … and to apologize as it had technically been her fault the ironstings had chased them.

Forgetown Square was busy with shoppers, and Picante's Pizza Parlour had put up pastel pink, yellow and blue bunting because part of the restaurant had been turned into an ice-cream shop for the summer.

Fenelda Spiggot waltzed into Picante's behind the two friends. "Hi, Cosmo!" she said, purposefully not making eye contact with Harley.

"Nel, if you're ignoring me because you think somehow that means you won't have to give me the golden light-bulb badge for my half of the summer, then think again." Last term Harley had eventually won the coveted Pupil of the Term prize ... except it had been a joint win with Fenelda, so they had to share the badge.

"Oh!" Fenelda feigned shock. "Harley Hitch, I didn't see you there. You do kind of blend in." She indicated Harley's hair with a pointed finger. "But you've at least helped me decide which ice cream I want." Fenelda pushed past and put a coin on the counter. "I'll have a triple strawberry whip, please, Mr Picante."

Harley shook her head. "Very funny. And you're pushing in. You always have to come first, don't you?"

Fenelda shrugged and Harley counted to ten in her head. Fenelda had been her rival ever since Fenelda had accused Harley of cheating in the cogflower competition years ago. Harley hadn't, of course, but the head teacher of Cogworks, Professor Fretshaw, had disqualified her anyway.

Mr Picante looked up. "No jumping the queue, Miss Spiggot."

Harley shrugged. "It's all right, Mr Picante. Cosmo and I are still deciding what we want anyway."

After Fenelda had breezed back outside with her overloaded triple cone, Harley and Cosmo ordered their ice creams and stepped back into the square, where they found a bench in the sun to sit on.

"This passionfruit ping is the best!" Harley

groaned with happiness. "Grandpa Eden said he'd given Mr Picante some passionfruit seeds the other day, and I'd thought at the time it was a bit odd that Mr Picante might want them for his pizzas, but now I know what they were really for! The cog-shaped wafer is a nice touch. How's your chocolate-and-raspberry double-up?"

Cosmo said something like "Yummy" through loaded lips.

They finished their ice creams in delicious silence while watching the people of Forgetown come and go. Lettice Bigley arrived with her robot rabbit, Coppertail, and waved as she headed for Picante's. Professor Horatio was helping Mrs Horatio in Bolting Blooms. Professor Anning was arranging an archaeology sandpit dig for toddlers outside the newly opened museum. Professor Spark was adjusting the clockwork cuckoo, and Rufus was outside Kitchen Imagine with his dad admiring the new display of electro-snapping scissors, his budgie-bot, Awk, flying excitedly above. Professors Maple and Twine were being helped by Harley's classmates Tarak and Henry, who were particularly good at art, to construct some sort of mini steam-engine installation in the middle of the square.

Harley loved her hometown. She waved at Delores, who was coming out of Cog Mill Bakery across the road with a cog pretzel as large as her head. Then she nudged Cosmo. "Hey, is that your mum over there by Cosmic Sewing? You said she wouldn't tell you what she's planning for the summer... I wonder what she's up to with that bag of paper rolls..."

"I don't know, but she'll tell me eventually. Harley, don't let your curiosity get the better—"

Harley gasped, jumping up. "Mr Bobbins is looking *very pleased* about whatever she's just said to him! Come on, let's find out!" She shoved the last of her ice cream into her mouth and hurried across the square towards Mrs Willoughby, with Cosmo not far behind.

"Hi, Mum," Cosmo mumbled.

Mrs Willoughby looked up. Her usually neat

hair had strands unpinned, and she'd misbuttoned her jacket. "Oh, hello, darling. I can't talk now. I've a million and one things to organize, and everyone at the council seems to think it's OK to take a holiday this week, so there was no one to help give out posters for the event!"

"We could help, Mrs Willoughby," Harley said, itching to know what it was about.

"Would you?" Mrs Willoughby looked at her keenly, and before Harley could confirm, she thrust the large bag of rolled-up posters into her arms. "Give one to every shopkeeper to put up, and tell them to make sure they're displayed prominently." She was already dashing away, mumbling about organization and health-and-safety nightmares. "And make sure you tell your Grandpa Elliot to come and see me!" she called back. "This is front-page news, and I need him to do a big story!"

"*What's* front-page news, Mum?" Cosmo shouted after her.

"Can't talk now! Love you, darling!" She was across the square in a moment and heading in the direction of the town hall.

Passing Cosmo the majority of the bundle, Harley kept one and swiftly unfurled it. Her heart leaped as she read:

FORGETOWN
The INVENTIA-WIDE famous

AVIATION
PARADE

Showcasing the MOST
MARVELLOUS
Flying wonders of Inventia
AUGUST
28th

"Whoa, Cosmo, this is epic! I can't believe this is coming to Forgetown! No wonder your mum's so busy. I've heard of the Aviation Parade, but never imagined we'd get the chance to see it right here. It's going to be HUGE for this town!"

"So *that's* what she's been so consumed by!"

Harley grabbed Cosmo's arm and squeezed excitedly.

"Ow!"

"It gets better! It also says there will be *a chance for local inventors to team up to design and display their own invented flying machines in a …*" Harley paused to absorb the utter wonder she felt at seeing the next words: "*… sky obstacle-course race with the theme 'Creatures of the Sky'. Let nature's wonders inspire your designs!*"

Fenelda, who was walking past with Lettice, snatched the poster from Harley.

"What's this? A competition?"

"Hi, Harley!" said Letti, smiling as Sprocket and Coppertail began happily chasing each other around the base of the clockwork cuckoo.

"Hi, Letti!" Harley was too full of joy at the news to be annoyed at Fenelda for snatching the poster. "Yes, Nel, it's a competition to invent and race a flying machine!" Harley turned to Cosmo. "This is exactly what I was saying we needed earlier – it's ambitious, it's epic, it's … right up my street!"

"It does sound exciting," Cosmo agreed. "But I thought you were looking forward to a summer of freedom and *not* planning."

"This changes everything!" Harley breathed. Sparks were already popping in her imagination. She'd never been able to see the Aviation Parade in real life before, as it was usually in some faraway part of Inventia, but Grandpa Elliot had shown her pictures of all the wonderful flying machines in copies of the *Inventia City Times* that his journalist friend in the city, Daphne Cringle, had sent him previous summers.

"What could we possibly come up with that would win a sky obstacle race?" Harley tapped her foot on the cobbles. They wouldn't have time to build something large, like the great airships she'd seen in the pictures; it would have to be small-scale and fast, and what creature of the sky could they base it on?

"Letti, join with me, won't you?" Fenelda said, grabbing Letti's hands. "It says we can work in teams. Delores! Come over and see this! You can join my team too!"

Harley didn't panic at Fenelda's rapid gathering of an inventing team. She worked perfectly well with Cosmo and the only thing she needed was a good idea. The *best* idea.

All manner of thoughts popped into her brain: mini helicopters made to look like dragonflies, gliders with bird wings, hoverboard bees…

She watched as Awk joined Sprocket and Coppertail, dashing around the square.

Then a fizzing sensation began to fill Harley. She looked at Cosmo, her cheeks blossoming red like ripe orchard apples. "I have an idea."

CHAPTER 4
RUSTY RIVER

The timing was almost too good to be true. Harley couldn't believe how everything had come together so beautifully in her mind in that moment.

A sky obstacle-course race was a *perfect* opportunity not only to invent something amazing but something that could double up and solve Cosmo's pet problem! The theme of Creatures of the Sky was brilliant – but Harley wasn't just going to create a flying transport that was *inspired* by creatures; she was going to create an actual flying creature! How cool would it be for Cosmo to have a *flying pet?*

He was going to love this!

It was as though a light bulb had turned on in her head. *Of course!* All robots in Inventia, including pets like Sprocket, had artificial intelligence (AI) brains that, basically, let them have their own thoughts. Harley was sure that no one had ever thought to create a transport that could think for itself – surely it would fly itself better than any pilot could!

Mrs Willoughby would be so impressed.

But she wasn't going to tell Cosmo her full plan, because it would be much more fun as a surprise.

"So you think we should create our flying machine in the shape of an actual *creature?*" Cosmo said doubtfully as they finished handing out the posters. He jogged beside her to keep up.

"Of course! The best designs copy nature closely, because nature has already worked everything out. The others will probably simply decorate their machines with the theme. I want us to go all in. And keep your voice down in case Fenelda starts spying to steal ideas."

"But wouldn't it be more practical to just put our own spin on a flying machine that already exists and add a few decorations like everyone else? The goal is to win the obstacle race, after all. Designing and building a totally new *creature* machine sounds overly ambitious."

"But *everyone else* will be mainly focusing on the flight mechanics. Not us! We're going to create something that flies but has *wild beauty*." Harley grinned widely at the thought of telling Cosmo at the finishing line that it was *actually a pet for him*. She imagined Mrs Willoughby rushing over to marvel at their creation. She would *have* to say yes to him keeping it, surely!

"It'll have to be something big enough to ride on," Cosmo mused. "But what?"

"I don't know, not yet. That's why we're heading to Rusty River. Sprocket, could you dash back to Hitch House to get the rod? We'll meet you there."

Rusty River was the place Harley always went to when she needed to work out her next move. It was a unique area where the water flowed orange from the Copper Mountains and wise robot fish swam upstream. Their advice was always mysterious, but Harley thought she had the knack for working it out.

As they approached the bridge that crossed the river, Sprocket sped down the lane with a fishing rod in his mouth.

They sat on the edge and cast the line, then waited.

"I suppose a large eagle might work," said Cosmo. "Or one of those huge gulls that live in the frozen seas in the far south of Inventia. Or an owl? I love owls."

"Perhaps." Harley frowned thoughtfully, not taking her eyes from the gently flowing water, keen for something to bite. She'd considered upscaling a smaller bird into a flying robot, but she couldn't decide which bird. She wanted something unique for Cosmo. She knew the fish from the Rusty River would prompt her in the right direction.

"As long as we don't choose the shape of an ironsting," said Cosmo, rubbing his backside.

It was thirty fidgeting, huffing and sighing minutes before Harley's line tugged. She knew it would be great advice now that she'd waited this long.

Reeling the line in, she was amazed to see she'd caught a robotic eel! "Wow, I didn't even know there *were* eels in the river!"

It slopped into her lap and wriggled to face her. Its skin was dark metal, and it fixed her with orange eyes.

"I'm ready for your wisdom," whispered Harley.

The eel spoke in a slimy, slithery voice. *"Reality is never as good as … your imagination."* After a lingering stare, it wriggled away and plopped back into the river with barely a splash.

"Er, that was about as useful as a jelly knife," said Cosmo, ruffling his hand through his curls.

"No, it *was* helpful," Harley insisted as she searched her mind to make the eel's words fit. "Reality is never as good as … your imagination," she whispered, as though the words were gold.

"Got it!" she shouted, almost making Cosmo fall into the river. "Next stop, the library!"

She thought it was a genius way of approaching the solution: the eel had basically told her not to look to reality but to imagine something even more amazing! And Cosmo had waited his whole childhood for a robot pet, so he deserved the very best, *most extraordinary* pet, something that would wow not only his mum but all the other children at Cogworks and win the obstacle race. Something legendary. She took the eel's message to mean that she needed to look beyond reality to the *creatures of mythology*, and there were bound to be books about them in Forgetown Library.

"Sometimes it would be good not to feel like the wash in the wake of your ideas," Cosmo puffed as he ran to catch up again.

"Sorry. I'm just excited." Harley was tempted to tell him the full truth of her plan, but she resisted. It would be worth waiting to see the look of happiness on his face at the parade. "Do you know if the library has a myths section?"

Cosmo helped out at the library on weekends. He nodded. "It's not a big section, but there are some stories."

"Is there anything on mythical creatures? Of the flying sort?"

"Oh, I see your plan! You think we could base our flying machine on something mythical?"

"Yes." *And to make you the coolest robot pet in the history of everything,* she thought to herself with a smile. "The eel practically told us that reality wasn't as good as imagined creatures."

"I still think it's a little over the top to make it an actual flying creature," said Cosmo. "Are you sure we shouldn't go straight to the engineering section and research small flying vehicles? We could just add bird wings, perhaps? What about something that uses a propeller? We could make it look like a flying insect and draw inspiration from seeds in nature. The way sycamore seeds travel like helicopter blades, for example, or the way dandelion seeds work like tiny parachutes…"

Harley shook her head. "It has to be an actual creature."

Cosmo shrugged as they walked through the library entrance. "OK, if you insist. The myth books are over there."

They passed Fenelda in the engineering section. Although they couldn't see her behind the shelves, her voice rang out: "We could use a turbine to create the flying machine's own wind in case it's a still day. Letti, you research that, and, Delores, you can sketch helicopter ideas while I work out how to add a small engine to a bicycle. I've got a spare one in the garage I can use. To make it look like a dragonfly, we can add bi-wings, and attach saucepan lids to the handlebars to look like the eyes."

Harley smiled to herself. Her actual creature was going to be much better.

The books on the shelf parted suddenly and Fenelda popped her head through.

"Nel, it's like you can sense me or something!"

Harley wondered if Fenelda had put some sort of tracking device on her.

"Oh, please, you clomp like an elephant in your big boots, and I caught a flash of your pink hair. But you should know *we've* already made a good start on our machine. You can't be that serious about winning the race if you're only starting your research now."

"I had thinking to do," Harley said haughtily. "Come on, Cosmo, let's work over here in peace."

Cosmo gave a little wave to Letti and Delores through the books and then hurried behind Harley to the myths section on the other side of the library.

After collecting an armful of the books that looked most interesting, they found a quiet corner for their research.

"These are incredible. There's an actual flying horse in this story!" said Harley, marvelling at the illustrations in one book.

"I never realized there were so many types of dragon in myths. There's something called a wyvern, which has two legs rather than four!"

Harley's eyes lit up at the thought, but then Cosmo shivered and said, "They look a bit scary and way too big for our machine."

They carried on scouring the books.

Cosmo showed her another creature. "Look, it's a rabbit with feathers for ears!"

"Cute, but not big enough to ride."

"Maybe we should just go for a giant eagle? Eagles are fascinating. Do you know they have amazing eyesight? Some can see five times further than a human. That's a cool fact, right?"

Harley smiled. She loved the way Cosmo's eyes lit up at the idea, but she wasn't convinced herself. "Eagles are real, and remember the eel put an emphasis on imagination." She wanted something even better, more outrageous, than an eagle.

Then Harley turned a page and gasped. It was more perfect than she could have hoped for: the ideal size for riding, and so different it would be certain to wow Mrs Willoughby – and everyone else.

"Stop the search!" she declared dramatically.

CHAPTER 5

INTENT

Harley turned the book to show Cosmo.

The legendary creature beautifully illustrated on the page had the front half of an eagle and the back half of a horse.

"A hippogriff?" he said, pushing his glasses up the bridge of his nose with a big grin. "Awesome!"

Harley could imagine Fenelda's face this autumn if she saw Cosmo flying to school on a hippogriff.

Cosmo read aloud: "They were once thought to be native to a small part of Inventia on the other side of the Copper Mountains and were incredibly shy. But no evidence of their existence has ever been uncovered."

"That's because they're a myth! But imagine how magnificent it'll be to bring one to life – making imagination better than reality, like the eel said."

"It would be impressive, I must admit. But don't forget, the goal is to win the obstacle race, so we may have to add things like propellers or balloons."

Harley was buzzing with the possibilities of creating a robot hippogriff that looked impressive and had all sorts of useful pet gadgetry for Cosmo. She didn't want balloons and propellers cluttering the outside because winning the race wasn't the most important thing. It was all about impressing Mrs Willoughby.

Harley felt quite proud of herself, really: for the first time, she wasn't focused on getting the glory of winning. Fenelda could have the victory she wanted so badly. Harley was happy to do something nice for Cosmo instead.

As the days, then weeks passed, the build-up and excitement for the parade grew steadily until the town was awash with colourful bunting, lanterns shaped like balloons, and groups of children and grown-ups working on their various flying contraptions in their gardens.

Cosmo hardly saw his mum as she prepared for the influx of visitors from across Inventia and made arrangements for the parade.

Harley insisted on him taking regular breaks from helping her so he could walk the streets of Forgetown and keep an eye on what everyone else was creating. That gave her opportunities to work on adding the important pet features that she wanted to keep a secret from Cosmo. He would certainly question the need for a hot-chocolate-maker in an obstacle race, for example...

They constructed their hippogriff in the garage, away from prying eyes. It was difficult spending so many days of the summer indoors, but Harley didn't want Fenelda getting wind of her creation. Fenelda would tell everyone and spoil the surprise for Mrs Willoughby. The only people Harley told were her grandpas. Grandpa Eden was great at mechanics and had helped her make lots of adjustments to Sprocket, and Grandpa Elliot could source unusual parts that couldn't be easily found in the Iron Forest – like the important AI processor – from his many contacts in Inventia.

"What's the update?" Harley asked Cosmo after

he returned from one of his trips into town. She glanced up through her protective goggles, a welder in hand.

"The same as yesterday. There are a variety of wings, blades and hover mechanisms, but no one is creating anything like our creature."

"Good. We're sure to stand out."

"And win the race?" said Cosmo.

"Of course!"

"Maybe tomorrow I could come and help with the wings in the morning rather than do yet another loop of the town?"

"They're almost done," Harley told him.

"What about the beak?"

"That reminds me: I need you to collect a package from Miss Li in town. A sound box from Inventia."

"Why does it need a sound box?"

"It's … to sound an alarm in case we're about to

crash into any obstacles," she fibbed. Really she had used a chunk of her savings to buy an eagle sound box so it could make some basic calls, similar to how Sprocket had a basic dog communication box.

"You could come with me this time and we could get another ice cream from Picante's?" suggested Cosmo. "It's a beautiful day out there…"

Without glancing up from the front claw she was busy soldering, she said, "I'm too busy. Take Sprocket."

The following day, Cosmo asked if he could help with the feathers.

"Yes, good idea. I need some more of the thin leaves from the silver oak. They're light and perfect for cutting into feathers... if you don't mind nipping to the Iron Forest for me. And can you go and see Rebelina at the junkyard and ask if she has any old parts we can make into the steering mechanism?"

She pretended not to notice Cosmo's exhale of frustration.

"It might be nice to actually help with what you're doing sometimes," he said as he left her to it.

*

Later, Cosmo returned with the parts she'd asked for. "Rebelina said this was the closest thing she had to a steering mechanism, but she has none of the right connectors and it's missing a chip."

"Thanks. I'll see what I can do with it," said Harley.

"Can I help with anything you're doing now?"

"Some strawberries from the greenhouse would be lovely. I'm famished."

"I meant on the hippogriff. The legs are looking great, by the way. Just like a horse's."

"Grandpa Eden helped me with the metal shaping last night."

"After I went home?" he said, the tone of disappointment evident. "I would have liked to have helped. Mum was working late again, so I ended up reading on my own."

"Hmm," Harley said, clearly not paying attention while she tinkered with the back knee joints.

"There are likely going to be loops to fly through, so I was thinking we could perhaps attach a small propeller to the tail. I started sketching—"

"I see what you're saying, but it'll spoil the look. Anyway, the wing joints will have small pistons for quick action."

The garage fell silent, and it was a short while before Harley picked up on the frosty atmosphere. "Is something the matter?" she asked eventually.

Cosmo's arms were folded as tight as sailors' knots. "Yes, actually, there is. This is meant to be a team effort and so far there seems to be only one member of our team: you. You keep sending me on errands, but it would be nice to feel a bit more included and do some of the actual work together."

Harley turned to her best friend. "Look, Cosmo,

we have different strengths, and we both want it to be perfect, right? And that reminds me, I need some more solder, so perhaps you could go and get that for me now, then tomorrow you could help? Actually, the day after," she added quickly, realizing she needed to do some crucial work on activating the robot brain. She was hoping the key part would arrive after Cosmo went home.

"Oh, forget it. I'm going back to my house to see if I can do some filing for Mum. It'll likely be more interesting."

"Don't be like that. I promise, soon it—"

"I'll pop back in a few days, if I can fit you in," he said sarcastically, then left the garage without looking back.

Staring at Harley with rain clouds in his eyes, Sprocket let out a disappointed whimper.

"I know it *sounds* like I'm ignoring his ideas,

Sprocket, but I can't let Cosmo get too close to the hippogriff now; it would spoil all the surprise pet features. Don't worry, he'll come back round when he realizes the hippogriff is a gift for him at the parade. He'll forgive me."

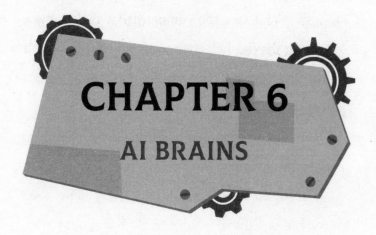

CHAPTER 6

AI BRAINS

It was two weeks until the parade. Cosmo stayed away, but Harley checked in with him on his digi-com, reassuring him that she still very much wanted him involved for the test flight. They could ride the hippogriff around the obstacle course together!

After dreams filled with flight, Harley hurried down to breakfast. "Any news on the AI part, Grandpa Eden?"

"There's a shortage of such parts," he told her. "Elliot's friend says the company that makes them have shut for the holidays, so if they didn't send it before they closed, it's unlikely you'll get your AI processor in time for the parade."

"But that's disastrous!" No processor meant no personality – and no pet for Cosmo!

"I'm sure it'll work out. It was a very clever idea to try, but you'll still be able to fly it without such a part. You can just control it yourself."

"I know, but..." She hadn't told Grandpa Eden about the *pet* part of her project, as she thought it would be nice to surprise everyone at once. Maybe she could get hold of a robot brain component herself somehow. "You're right. It'll be fine. I'm going back to work on the hippogriff some more."

"Isn't Cosmo coming to help today? I haven't seen him much lately."

"He's coming over for the test flight in a couple of days," Harley called, hurrying out of the kitchen.

But instead of heading to the garage, Harley followed the path to the Iron Forest. Perhaps luck would be on her side and she would find something growing there that would work. She kept her fingers crossed as she entered the forest and began scanning the branches above, then rooting through the fuse ferns below.

"Sprocket, use your super scent to detect anything unusual."

His nose began flashing red. He put it to the ground and started sniffing along the forest floor. They hunted for an hour and Harley was about to give up when Sprocket's tail began wagging double time.

"You've sensed something! What is it, boy?"

He led her past a line of tall needle pines, through a thick patch of fuse ferns and then...

"Stop! Sprocket, it's a patch of oil pods!"

Oil pods were treacherous, low-lying plants that exploded with thick oil if anything touched them. Sprocket had rolled in them on several occasions and would again if given the chance.

Doing as he was told, Sprocket sat at the edge of the patch, his tail wagging even more quickly now. Then Harley saw it. Sprocket wasn't just seeking out the oil pods; in the centre of the patch was a strange cresting bloom. Grandpa Eden had once told her that oil-pod patches only flowered one day a year, when the conditions were perfect. The bloom was a metallic bright yellow flower that looked remarkably like a little brain!

"Are you seeing what I'm seeing?" she asked Sprocket. "If I could reach it, it would be worth a try as the hippogriff's brain! Grandpa Eden always says the Iron Forest has a habit of knowing what you

66

need when you need it, and this looks like the very thing for our robot!"

She reached forward. Frustratingly, it was too far away.

"Maybe I can step between the pods if I stay on tiptoes."

Sprocket tilted his head as though to say, *But*

you never let me *play in the oil pods!* The viscous oil inside the pods was nearly impossible to wash off without special materials. She wouldn't want to get oil on the strange brain flower and damage that either.

Harley planned her route. "You stay here, Sprocket. Don't move a paw."

He gave a disappointed whine but understood.

With ballet-dancer precision, Harley lifted a foot and placed her toes in the small space between pods, knowing any little knock would activate them. Carefully, she transferred her weight forward and aimed for a small gap with her other foot. As she did, a bright blue butterfly flew towards her. Trying to ignore it, she focused on her footwork and just made the gap as the butterfly landed on her nose.

"Not helpful," she said, relieved that she was somehow managing to stay on her tiptoes. "I'm not

a flower, so if you could be on your way, I have a mission to complete." She jutted out her bottom lip and blew upwards so that the butterfly flew away.

"Right, onwards we go." Harley took a deep breath, then edged ahead. Her hands cupped the flower at the exact moment that she heard an excited *yip* from Sprocket. She glanced over her shoulder. "No! Don't chase the—"

It was too late. The springs in Sprocket's legs gave a merry *boing* as he leaped towards the butterfly and on to the patch. The oil pods exploded.

Harley thrust herself forward to protect the flower as best she could as gooey black oil splattered across her bare skin, into her hair and all over her clothes. As she hit the ground, more pods detonated like little bombs, until she was covered from head to toe.

Oblivious, Sprocket was now rolling happily

in the oil beside her, while the butterfly, which had somehow avoided the splatter of oil, flitted off, a bright blue speck flying towards the next plant.

Harley rolled on to her back and peeked inside her still-cupped hands. "At least the flower's still clean!"

Luckily, Grandpa Eden had a good supply of oil diffuser flowers and leaves at home.

"Whatever were you doing to end up like this?" He brushed the feathery white flower across her face, and it sucked up the oil like magic, turning grey-black as it did.

"I needed a part for the hippogriff, then Sprocket saw a butterfly and set off the oil pods."

"No harm done. We'll soon have you cleaned up."

It took over an hour, then Grandpa Eden said

Harley could carry on with her invention while he cleaned Sprocket.

As she opened the garage door and the sunlight streamed inside, she couldn't help but think how utterly splendid the hippogriff looked, and it wasn't even moving yet. The wing shape looked like that of an eagle, and the silver feathers shone magnificently. It had taken weeks to craft all the feather details and they sparkled in the light. The hippogriff was roughly the size of a pony, and big enough to sit both her and Cosmo on its back. She'd finished adding turbos to the rear horse legs so that it could get an impressive run-up to take flight, and Grandpa Eden had helped her put the eyes in. She'd decided to go for realistic-looking eyes that were also cameras for taking in information. The many delicate metal feathers concealed the various compartments and sensors well, and made the creature look so lifelike.

Harley unhitched the beak and lifted it open to access the inner working panels and wires inside the head. She took the brain flower from her bag and began carefully attaching wires. She was hopeful it would work. When she was satisfied that all the wires were hooked up as she thought they should be, she carefully shut the beak.

"Here goes nothing." She took a breath and flipped a switch. "Hello, hippogriff!"

Nothing happened.

"Welcome to Inventia. I'm Harley Hitch, and…" She suddenly felt daft for talking to an inanimate chunk of metal, no matter how lifelike it looked.

She sighed. The flower from the Iron Forest had been worth a try, but she'd have to wait for the package to arrive from Inventia City after all – and just hope it would arrive in time for the parade. If it didn't, at least they would be able to activate the hippogriff in basic mode in order to race. But the whole point of building it had been to make a surprise pet for Cosmo, one that would be super impressive with its artificial intelligence.

Then she heard the faintest of whirring noises coming from the hippogriff's head.

Its eyes opened and illuminated yellow.

"Yes!" Harley exclaimed, punching the air with her fist. "You're working! I didn't doubt it for a second."

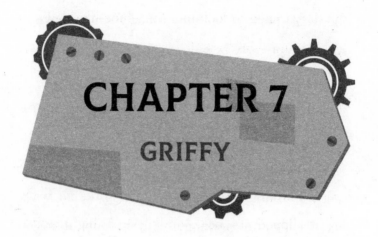

CHAPTER 7

GRIFFY

After spending time activating simple voice commands to extend the wings and take different steps around the garage, Harley noticed the creature's personality developing quickly. At first it was tentative, but it was soon emitting high-pitched, robotic whistles and responding to her commands.

The glow of success was a huge, happy balloon in her chest. "Cosmo is going to be over the moon! We'll need to do some tricks at the parade to impress his mum, but I'll keep you on command-only mode for now. You need to look more machine-like and less pet-like until the obstacle race, do you understand?"

It gave a curious tilt of its head.

"To make it easy for you, I've programmed your circuits so that when I say 'command only', your brain goes silent, and when I say 'brain activate', your pet features switch back on, OK?"

It dipped its beak and gave a high-pitched whistle-chirp.

"Cosmo will give you a proper name, so you can just be Griffy for now. And you seem like a girl hippogriff, is that right?"

Griffy dipped her head, nodding.

"We'll try your flying skills when it gets dark. All the others will be testing their machines by now and I don't want them to see you."

Griffy gave another nod.

"Good – but there is the small problem of getting Cosmo over here. He's not exactly happy with me at the moment." Harley took her digi-com from her pocket. "Cosmo, come in. Cosmo, are you there?" He usually answered within seconds. "Cosmo, it's time for a test flight. Are you there?"

"Ah, so you remember who I am now?" his voice finally replied.

"Sorry. I'm going to make it up to you, I promise, and I have my reasons. You'll just have to trust me. Our machine is ready for a test flight tonight."

"Are you sure you wouldn't rather fly it alone?"

"No, don't be silly." *This is all for you*, she thought. "Come on, you can't stay annoyed at me forever. I'll get my grandpas to speak to your mum so you can stay over. We can get pizza and ice cream."

His voice softened. "All right, I'll see you soon. Bye."

Harley grinned at Griffy. "You're going to

love being Cosmo's pet. And wait until you meet Sprocket! But for now ... *command only.*"

Harley heard Cosmo coming down the path whistling like a bird. She rushed to open the garage door. When Cosmo saw the hippogriff trotting robotically around the garage, it was as if he'd never been annoyed at Harley. "I have to admit, I was dubious about this from the start, but it's incredible!"

"I'm so happy you like it. There's more to come too."

"I can't wait to see it fly!" said Cosmo.

"Me neither!"

But they did have to wait; they waited until after dinner. As the sun set, Harley and Cosmo, along with Harley's grandpas, led the hippogriff to the hill behind Cogworks school for a test run.

"A low flight at first, please," said Grandpa Elliot. "Take it easy, in case of mishaps."

"No more than a quick run-up and a few metres off the ground," added Grandpa Eden, passing them helmets he'd insisted on bringing.

The pair secured their helmets and mounted the robot hippogriff.

"Here we go!" said Harley. "She's programmed for basic flight moves, so we can give simple commands like 'take off' and—"

With that, the hippogriff took several strides and flapped its wings. They lifted from the ground.

"Stay low," she added swiftly. "Fly in a circle."

Her heart raced. It was working perfectly!

Cosmo held on tight as the hippogriff followed the commands. "She's fabulous!" he called out.

After banking clockwise, Harley instructed the creature to do another low loop before landing beside her grandpas.

"Wonderful!" said Grandpa Elliot. "You've done

a brilliant job, both of you."

"It was all Harley, really," said Cosmo.

"Grandpa Eden did lots too," she said, still feeling bad about leaving Cosmo out.

As they led the hippogriff home from the Cogworks hill, Harley noticed that the stars on the low horizon looked more twinkly than usual. She wondered if her friends from the star-chatter observatory had come down for a closer look. Then she realized it was probably something else – she took her small telescope from her belt.

The lights were part of some sort of airship. "It's the Aviation Parade! They're on their way!"

"I do believe you're right!" said Grandpa Eden. "How exciting. Let's get you both tucked up in bed so you can see them first thing in the morning."

*

Harley barely slept. It was all going brilliantly, and she couldn't wait for parade day and the big reveal. She was awake the moment the orange brush of sunrise lit her window. She hurriedly dressed and knocked for Cosmo, who was in the spare room next door, then called "Wake up!" to her grandpas.

They all talked excitedly over breakfast.

"I can't wait to see the different machines fly into town," said Harley, grabbing a pastry.

"They'll save them for parade day," said Grandpa Elliot.

"Won't we see them all fly in?" she asked.

Grandpa Elliot shook his head. "Each year the machines are different, and they'll have a clever way of making it a surprise."

Harley stuffed the rest of her croissant in her mouth, listening eagerly.

"The flying contraptions always look marvellous in the pictures, but it'll be something else to see them in real life," said Grandpa Elliot.

"Do you think many people will come for parade day?" asked Cosmo.

"Thousands!" said Grandpa Eden.

Harley grinned. "So there'll be a *huge* audience for the obstacle course race too?"

Cosmo almost choked on his pastry. "Thousands? Really?"

The idea thrilled Harley. She downed her orange juice. "I can hear rumbling. I think they're close." She was so excited she almost squealed. She dropped her plate in the sink and grabbed her coat. "Come on!"

Outside, a distant chugging pulsed the air. Harley searched the sky. "Where are they?"

"Have patience. Jumping around won't make

them arrive more quickly," said Grandpa Eden, closing the door.

"Let's head up the hill."

As the chug grew louder, Harley could hear the banging of doors as various neighbours came outside to look too.

Cosmo whistled loudly as they walked up the slope.

"Cosmo!" Harley shot him a glare. "I know you're excited, but you're distracting me from the engine sound! You're not even very tuneful."

"I was just—"

"Shh! I can see something under that huge cloud!"

Then, above the morning gleam of the Iron Forest, a huge pointed shape appeared.

"It looks like a giant spear!" Harley couldn't imagine what it could be. Then a second point appeared far to the left, then another.

"Wait, it's some sort of roof... A turret!" she exclaimed.

"You're right!" said Cosmo.

Harley's eyes widened. "It's like an enormous castle rising in the sky! That's impossible, though..."

"Impossible is often just something you've never seen before," said Grandpa Elliot, smiling.

Cosmo jabbed his finger at the sky. "That's not a cloud – it's a huge balloon! It *is* a flying castle!"

"It's gigantic!" gasped Harley. "Wait, the rest is coming into view. Look at all the ropes and that incredible round window!"

A blast of fiery air illuminated the towers of the flying castle, which was big enough to fill Forgetown Square.

By now every person in town was in the streets watching the magnificent building fly over the Iron Forest, casting a vast, sweeping shadow below. As it neared, they could see people waving from the castle turrets. They waved back and watched as it flew onwards.

"Where will it land?"

"Probably the field close to the Rusty River. It's flat there, and there's enough space," said Grandpa Eden.

They jogged, following it down the path to the field, and came upon Mrs Willoughby wearing a luminous yellow jacket and waving two fluorescent sticks in the air. She looked flustered.

"Keep behind the barriers," she ordered.

The stream of arriving townspeople crowded close by as the balloon castle decelerated and began a slow descent towards the field. With impressive precision, the lower building touched the ground and the balloon began folding into the main castle structure as it enveloped it and also touched down.

The ground rumbled and the people of Forgetown clapped and cheered.

"This is going to be epic!" breathed Harley.

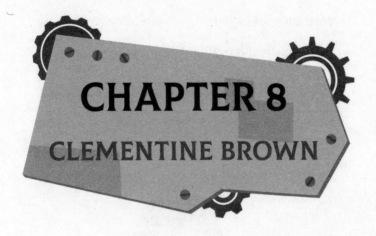

CHAPTER 8
CLEMENTINE BROWN

A small door opened at the bottom of the castle and out strode the most impressive woman Harley had ever seen. She wore a leather jacket glimmering with brass buttons, and a thick belt around her waist with buckle wings in gold. A glimpse of red fringe could be seen beneath a tight brown aviator hat with circular coverings over the ears, and round flying goggles were perched on her forehead. The woman's large eyes were lined with black, giving her a feline appearance and she wore striking brown lipstick.

Harley decided that when she was older she would be just like this woman, whoever she was.

"Clementine Brown," said the woman as she approached Mrs Willoughby with a hand outstretched. "I'm the captain of the flying

castle and manager of the Aviation Parade. We're thrilled to bring the parade to your wonderful town this year. I've long wanted to visit the Iron Forest and Rusty River, so I jumped at the opportunity when you submitted the application to host."

"I'm Wanda Willoughby, the councillor who has made all the arrangements. A warm welcome to Forgetown. We're delighted to have you here."

"Thank you for your hard work and the detailed town maps," said Clementine. "It helped enormously in planning the obstacle course for the race. Did you receive the proposal?"

"Indeed, and I've arranged all the equipment you asked for."

"We've never thought to include a race for inventive attendees before. It'll be a fun warm-up to the main parade. Forgetown has quite the reputation for producing young talent!" Her eyes met Harley's and she flashed a smile.

"Indeed, we do," Mrs Willoughby said proudly. "The residents are beyond excited. You have a few days to rest – Forgetown Hotel is completely blocked out for your aviators, and Picante's, our town restaurant, is ready to host you for breakfast, when you and your crew are ready. Their cannoli and coffee are the finest in Inventia."

"Fabulous! I like it here already. Are you sure about the hotel? We're more than happy to sleep in the castle."

Mrs Willoughby shook her head. "Absolutely not. The staff are eager to look after you all and provide anything you need. We've set up a shuttle land train from Inventia City to transport people in on the day of the parade. Anything you need, just ask."

"Wonderful."

Harley observed everything from the barrier with hungry concentration. "Where are the other flying machines?" she asked her grandpas.

"I expect they're all inside the castle," said Grandpa Elliot. "It's big enough to house a village!"

Clementine Brown marched forward with Mrs Willoughby, and Harley was about to say hello when Fenelda jumped in front of her.

"Welcome to Forgetown, Miss Brown." Fenelda presented Clementine with a bunch of cogflowers, before glancing at Harley and giving her a sly grin.

"She chose those on purpose, to wind me up," Harley whispered to Cosmo.

"Don't worry about her," he whispered back. "She's only annoyed because she hasn't been able to find out anything about your flying machine. She was very persistent with her questions."

"Thanks for not letting anything slip. You're the

best of friends, Cosmo." She smiled, and her heart blossomed at the thought of what his expression would look like when he found out the hippogriff was actually a gift for him. Mrs Willoughby was still stiff-shouldered and obviously tense about the arrangements, but come the day of the parade, when all the organizing was done, Harley would impress her with the hippogriff and everything would fall into place.

A stream of aviators began leaving the castle, chatting and smiling at the crowds as they walked. They all wore various leather jackets, hats and goggles, gloves, belts and buckles.

Harley looked on in awe. "We joke about running off to join the circus, but do you think it's possible to run off and join the castle?"

"Not yet, miss," said Grandpa Eden. "You've still got a few school years to complete! Come on, time for a brew. There's only so much excitement I can take in a morning."

The grandpas started back up the path home, but Harley and Cosmo lingered, watching Clementine Brown and her aviators head towards town.

"I have the obstacle-course plans," whispered the sing-song voice of Fenelda in Harley's ear.

Harley whipped round to face her. "You do not!"

"You're not the only one with secrets. Although I suspect the reason you've been so quiet about your machine is that you're probably a little bit embarrassed. Did it explode? Such unfortunate things tend to happen to you," Fenelda said, laughing lightly. "Maybe you should dye your hair black next time, then the soot won't show."

"Leave her alone, Fenelda," said Cosmo.

Harley didn't need Cosmo to stick up for her as she let Fenelda's comments slide off her like water

off a velocipede's back. She could see it for what it was: Fenelda's problem, not hers. Nonetheless, she was proud of Cosmo for challenging Fenelda, and she gave him a grin. He wouldn't have been brave enough to do that last year.

"You can't have the plans because only Mrs Willoughby does, and she would show them to Cosmo before she would ever show you."

"My parents are close friends with her." Fenelda tapped her nose knowingly. "See you on parade day. If you're not too embarrassed by whatever failure of a machine you've attempted."

"You'll be eating your words, Nel Spiggot," Harley said breezily, and she linked Cosmo's arm and strode away, doing her best to lift her chin in the assured way Clementine Brown did and walking with the same purposeful stride.

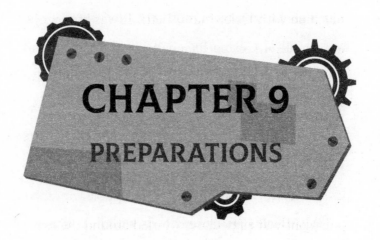

CHAPTER 9
PREPARATIONS

The next day, strange constructions started appearing around Forgetown: a large hoop on the Cogworks' roof, tall poles tied with ribbons at various points, wind socks, flags, ropes between trees, and cordoned-off areas for the crowds. Poor Mrs Willoughby looked more harassed than ever, so Cosmo and Harley joined the many volunteers in setting up the hundreds upon hundreds of spectator seats and a stage by the castle.

Harley caught sight of Fenelda trying out her machine with Delores and Letti. It was annoyingly impressive: small and agile, and they'd used part of a bike, with two enclosed helicopter-like blades above and thrusters behind the driver's seat. The controls were dual-sided – one on either side for each hand so each rotating blade could be controlled independently – and they'd given it double wings like a dragonfly. It zipped and whirled around the sky.

"Maybe we should get a bit more practice in," suggested Cosmo.

"But I don't want anyone to see it until the race tomorrow." Harley reminded herself that although winning would be the icing on the cake, the most important thing was to impress Mrs Willoughby – and right now Cosmo's mum wasn't in the best state of mind for that to happen. "Let's get an ice cream from Picante's and ignore Fenelda's showing-off."

"But we've only just had breakfast!"

"You do know there's a separate pudding stomach."

Cosmo shook his head hopelessly. "There is not."

Harley grinned. "Come on, we can get another look at all the other aviators on the way."

The town was already starting to fill with visitors. Many of the residents were renting out rooms, and a campsite had been set up in the fields behind the town. Small airship-shaped balloons hung from every lamp post, and Picante's had changed their entire menu to aviation-themed food, with kite wafers for the ice cream and pizzas shaped like hot-air balloons with wicker baskets filled with oregano-seasoned chips.

As the day wore on, Harley and Cosmo took their baskets of chips down to the site of the flying castle to watch as a great trapdoor was released at the back and various flying contraptions were wheeled from within to be oiled and polished in the sun.

Clementine Brown noticed their curiosity and approached the two friends. "Would you two like to help with my machine?"

Harley nearly fainted with shock that she had spoken to them. "Really?"

"Sure thing. You're Wanda's boy, right? She tells me you're working on a top-secret machine yourselves for the race, so you must be pretty good at mechanics. I can't wait to see what you've come up with."

Harley felt so happy she thought her cheeks must be glowing.

"Come on, then," said Clementine. "You can't help from behind the barrier."

They followed her towards the castle where a beautiful, sleek transporter was being wheeled out. It was old-fashioned, like the original fancy transporters Harley had seen in a museum years ago, but it looked sturdy and modern too, with all manner of silver pipes and fluted attachments.

"That doesn't look as though it'll fly," said Cosmo tentatively.

"Looks can be deceiving. Razor holds the record for the fastest sky machine in Inventia," Clementine told them. "It shaved a full twenty seconds off the previous record."

Harley was stunned. "But how?"

"She might look like an old dear, but she's actually packed with powerful technology. See these outlets? They're for jet rockets, and these two compartments in the side pop open at the touch of a button to reveal wings."

"It's a flying transporter!"

"Fun, isn't it?"

"Could the jet rockets make it to *space*?" It was Harley's life ambition to one day design a machine that could fly among the stars and planets. She loved chatting to the stars at the observatory, but to visit them in the sky and to look down on Inventia and see it as they did? That would be an absolute dream come true.

"It's not *that* powerful." Clementine laughed. "But I like your ambition." She passed them both a buffing cloth. "Come on. You can help me get her shining like a new penny for tomorrow, both inside and out."

Harley was impressed that Clementine worked just as hard as the rest when it came to polishing and oiling. Other aviators helped with cleaning the filters and adjusting the valves, and Clementine went over to help others in turn too. They all worked as a big team. Harley felt a terrible pang of guilt at how she'd treated Cosmo this summer, making all the hippogriff decisions herself. Even though she'd thought she needed to keep things secret for race day, maybe it would have been better to involve him after all?

"Hey, Cosmo, I really am sorry about excluding you."

Cosmo gave a nod of acknowledgement. "It's more fun working together, right?"

"Definitely."

By the time the sun was setting, they felt almost

as if they were part of the aviation squad, and were on first-name terms with most of the team. It felt like the best day of her life, and Harley knew it was only going to get better tomorrow.

Weary and satisfied, they eventually said goodbye and made their way back home.

"See you in the morning, Cosmo. We need to register for the race and pick up the course map first thing."

"See you tomorrow." Cosmo yawned.

She bent down to pat Sprocket. "Parade and surprise day. I can't wait!"

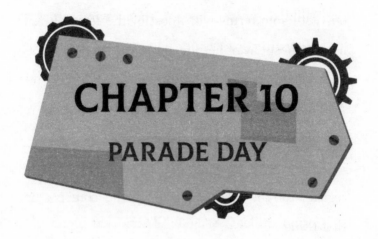

CHAPTER 10

PARADE DAY

Conditions for parade day were perfect with a light breeze and sapphire sky. Harley and Cosmo were first in the queue to register for the race. Eagerly unfurling the obstacle course map, they began memorizing the layout. The race would happen before the main parade. Harley was glad of that, because it meant she and Cosmo would be able to relax afterwards and enjoy the show.

"The starting line is at the bottom of town beside Cog Mill Bakery," said Harley, "then it winds around the star-chatter observatory, where it says we have to weave between two sky poles, past the crowds and through the hoop on top of the old mill, under the banner hanging between the two tall oaks of the Iron Forest, and then the finish line is through the hoop on top of Cogworks."

Cosmo smiled. "Brilliant! Then we'd better get the hippogriff flying machine ready."

"Where will your mum be seated?"

"Why?"

"No reason, particularly, I just want to make sure she gets a good view of us going past."

"She'll be in the VIP area here on the map. She's saved us seats for the parade afterwards."

"Great. Oh, look!" Harley pointed as the giant first-place trophy was lifted on to a display for the parade visitors to see. It was gold and in the shape of an airship.

"Do you think we practised enough?" Cosmo's voice had a small wobble to it.

"It'll be fine," she answered, steadying her own voice as she caught sight of Rufus tinkering with his winged bat machine, and Asma heaving an impressive set of butterfly wings and propeller on to her back.

Maybe her flying animal wouldn't be as unique as she'd imagined? But she pushed the thought away. Griffy could think for herself. She was different and ready to impress.

Back at the garage, Harley and Cosmo bumped into the grandpas, who were dressed up in bow ties for the occasion.

"Sprocket can sit with us while you fly," said Grandpa Elliot.

"Good luck, and make sure you both wear the helmets I gave you," said Grandpa Eden. "And remember, today is about fun. Let Fenelda Spiggot be competitive if she wants to; you just have a blast and get around safely."

"Ready, Cosmo?" asked Harley as she activated the battery switch on the hippogriff. A soft whirr sounded inside.

"As I'll ever be!" he replied.

"Then let's ride the hippogriff into town and make an entrance no one will forget."

Harley secured the saddle and leaned towards the microphone in Griffy's neck. "Command only."

"What did you say?" Cosmo frowned.

"Oh, just setting it to the right mode."

They led the hippogriff out into the sunshine. Her golden front eagle claws and beak gleamed, and the silver feathers glistened like diamonds.

"Here. Grandpa Eden said we can use the tri-wheel trundle bike goggles he uses on windy days. They're a bit tinted so will stop the glare. I've got these, and you can use his spare set."

"Thanks."

As they approached the crowds, everyone stopped and stared in awe at their metal creature.

"Wow, is that real?" asked a young girl.

"It's our entry for the race, so not exactly real," Cosmo answered, and Harley couldn't help a silent grin to herself knowing Griffy was so much more. She'd decided to activate the AI brain at some point during the race so it would be able to show off some spectacular flying. Then, after they had Mrs Willoughby's attention, Harley would complete her plan by revealing the creature's secret at the end of the race.

They began to head to the starting line where numerous flying machines were waiting, ready to go.

Fenelda looked as though she'd been forced to eat an onion when she saw them approach on the hippogriff. "You always have to be extra, don't you, Harley Hitch?" She shook her head and tutted.

"Impressive, isn't it?"

Fenelda didn't answer, but Letti, Delores and a flock of others rushed over to marvel at the hippogriff.

"That's amazing!"

"Wish I'd thought of that!"

"It's a mythical hippogriff!"

"Brilliant!"

Clementine Brown strode over and admired the mechanical creature. "Wow, I might have to offer you two a permanent job at the Aviation Parade! But the race is due to start soon, so get ready."

Harley rode the hippogriff to the starting line, to a free spot beside Fenelda's transport.

"I'm still going to win," Fenelda whispered.

Harley shrugged, but of course the comment irked her.

The last nervous minutes ticked by as everyone made their final preparations. A sea of people lined the distance, ready to cheer them on.

Harley and Cosmo remounted the hippogriff as the ten-second countdown began.

"Fly free but safely!" called Clementine. "On your marks, get set, go!"

A golden flare shot into the sky.

Everything erupted into action. Engines whirred, wings extended, balloons inflated.

Harley grasped the hippogriff's reins. "Take flight!"

Griffy's wings unfurled and she took several powerful steps. With two beats of her wings, they were rising.

"Woohoo!" Harley cried out.

"Tell it to bank left towards the observatory and head for the green flag!" Cosmo instructed.

"Bank left!"

Professor Twine shot past on some sort of feathered sky windsurfer with a yellow beak foot pedal, and Asma twirled high with her butterfly wings, but Fenelda's dragonfly-heli-bike was annoyingly swift and took first place from the off.

"Go higher so we don't hit that bat machine," Cosmo called. "As long as we don't go above the very top of the poles we'll still be on the course."

Harley instructed the hippogriff to ascend.

The crowds went wild with cheers as the small flying machines approached. Some contraptions ran out of steam and broke away from the flock straight away: Asma caught a wing on the pole and spun to the floor like a spinning top, and Professor Twine's sky windsurfer started sparking, so he had to set off his parachute and land swiftly.

"Bank left, bank right!" Harley instructed as the hippogriff glided between the poles. Mrs Willoughby would come into sight any moment, surely watching them with awe. Harley squinted at the crowds, hoping to pick her out.

"Concentrate, Harley! We need to make it

through the great hoop on the old mill or we'll be disqualified!" shouted Cosmo.

Harley felt a shudder, and she glanced over to see that Fenelda had bumped them from the side.

"Watch where you're going!" Fenelda called with a smile.

"Left a bit," Harley instructed the hippogriff, then looked back to the VIP seating at the front of the crowds. Mrs Willoughby was there, but she was busily waving her hands and talking on her digi-com. She wasn't even watching the race!

Harley needed to get her attention. At that moment, Fenelda dived through the hoop ahead of them and the crowd gave a cheer.

Normal flying wasn't going to be enough. It was time to activate the AI brain so the hippogriff could do something to definitely draw her attention.

"Mrs Willoughby!" Harley yelled. "Watch this!"

CHAPTER 11

ACTIVATE

"Activate brain!" Harley instructed.

"What are you talking about?" Cosmo called from behind. "That's not in the instruction list!"

The hippogriff seemed to relax as Harley's instruction initiated the shift to using Griffy's own brain. The creature's body undulated more freely now and her speed increased.

"Harley, this feels different. What have you

done?" Cosmo's hands clamped Harley's waist like two vices.

"Surprise, happy new pet day!" They shot through the hoop and were gaining on Fenelda.

"What do you mean? Whoa, slow down! My stomach needs to catch up!"

But at next glance Mrs Willoughby was still engrossed in her digi-com conversation. Fenelda was already heading under the banner between the iron oaks. Harley knew she had to either carry on with the course and risk Mrs Willoughby missing the whole spectacle or do something drastic.

"Do something impressive, Griffy!" she ordered, the words coming out of her mouth before she had time to think, and the hippogriff suddenly inclined vertically upwards.

"Nooooooooooooooo!" Cosmo yelled. "What's it doing?"

"We're clipped in. Just hold on – aghhhhh!"

Griffy let out a screech so high and loud it must have reached the Copper Mountains.

Up and up they went, the hippogriff screeching and spinning like a whirlpool. Then to her horror, Harley realized they were about to turn upside down. "Hold on!" she managed through tight lips as her cheeks were pushed back with the force. For a moment her heart felt so light she thought it had leaped from her chest. All of a sudden, Forgetown was the wrong way up, then they were falling in a vertical dive, leaving her stomach somewhere only clouds should be. They hurtled towards the ground.

"Bank up! Bank up!" Harley yelled. The hippogriff seemed to be out of control, and Harley tugged on the reins with every ounce of strength she could muster. Then the silver hippogriff screeched and pulled up, but only barely in time.

Somehow through the blur of faces, Harley caught Mrs Willoughby's look of horror as she saw them and dropped her digi-com. The crowd gasped as one as the hippogriff's wings faltered and the creature started to career through the sky like a blindfolded chicken being chased by a fox. Griffy juddered from side to side, then dipped towards the crowd, missing them by inches.

People began screaming, panicking and running in all directions. Harley barely managed to keep control of the reins and steered the hippogriff to the side, away from any people. Griffy's wing brushed the grass before she was up again, flying in startled zigzags in all directions. The hot-chocolate spout sprang from the side and brown liquid sprayed like rain on the spectators below.

"What is that?!" yelled Cosmo. "Harley, do something!"

"It's out of control!"

"Anything!"

She thought if she could just steer Griffy east, perhaps they could release their buckles and jump to safety in the Rusty River...

"Right, right, right!" she bellowed.

The hippogriff hurtled on like a living roller coaster, but they were almost above the river. Harley unclipped them and reached behind for Cosmo's hand. "Jump!"

The pair dropped into the orange water like two boulders. Harley kicked for the surface and took a gasp of air and spun to see Cosmo doing the same. They swam together towards the nearest bank.

"Are you all right?" she asked.

"I am. Are you?"

"Yeah, but I'm not sure about the hippogriff," said Harley.

Griffy was still shooting through the air, not knowing where to go and what to do, and the crowd's alarmed shouting only seemed to be making her more confused.

A robot eel popped its head through the surface of the water beside Harley. She recognized it as the same eel as before.

"What's the point of asking for advice if you don't listen?" it said slimily, shaking its head.

"I did! You told me that reality is never as good as your imagination."

"Exactly. The reality before you isn't quite how you'd imagined it would go, is it?"

"But I thought you meant to use my imagination more and to give the creature thought, as in *a brain*!" Harley huffed, then swam to the bank where Cosmo was waiting.

Clementine Brown hurried towards them with

Grandpa Elliot and Grandpa Eden close behind.

"Goodness, are you both all right?" she asked.

But before they could answer, a chorus of screeches echoed around them. They all looked towards the sound, seeing ten or so small grey dots appear in the distant sky, rapidly flying their way. As the objects neared, their details came into view: feathered wings and head, yellow beak and claws, strong hind legs with hooves.

"Good hippo-grief!" exclaimed Harley.

"Are they what I think they are?" said Cosmo, aghast.

"But hippogriffs are mythical!" said Grandpa Elliot.

They watched in utter shock as a flock of hippogriffs circled above.

Harley stood up, still dripping from the river. "What are they doing?"

"They seem to be gathering around your robot," said Clementine.

They circled the robot hippogriff and beat their wings in unison, decelerating. It seemed to quell Griffy's panic, and she began mimicking them, slowing her wings to a regular beat.

"They're calming her down!" said Grandpa Eden.

Then one of the hippogriffs broke the circle and began leading the others away from Forgetown, towards the Copper Mountains, while another hippogriff flew beside the robot so their wings almost touched, with a second hippogriff taking the other side.

"They're guiding her away!" Harley couldn't believe what she was seeing.

Soon the hippogriffs became specks again and all that could be seen of Griffy was a small flash of silver in the far distance.

CHAPTER 12

DEBRIEF

The main parade was called off. The crowds were calmed and eventually dispersed.

Clementine sat Harley and Cosmo beside the castle, wrapped them in towels and made them some sweet honey tea.

"You're both still in one piece, at least," said Grandpa Elliot. "Grandpa Eden is heading over to find Mrs Willoughby now to reassure her you're all right, Cosmo. She's being swarmed by the crowds, by the looks of it."

Harley had never felt so dreadful and miserable about her actions in all her life. Grandpa Elliot shook his head and put a consolatory hand on her shoulder. "It'll be all right. I'll go and help Eden and be back soon."

Clementine passed them the tea.

"I'm so sorry," Harley said. "I've ruined the parade and poor Mrs Willoughby's hard work, I've lost Griffy, and…" She had to stop because a sob shook her shoulders.

"Now, now," said Clementine. "If there's one thing I know about life, it's that things occasionally don't go to plan."

"But the parade had barely started, and all the people were so looking forward to seeing your amazing airships, and—"

"I once accidentally set fire to my hair when I overloaded with jet fuel, and another time I had to do an emergency landing in the Zinctile Plains after a booster malfunction."

Harley knew that Clementine was just trying to make her feel better, and it made her like her even more, which then made Harley feel so incredibly disappointed in herself that she tucked her head into her knees and sobbed again. Sprocket whimpered and licked her ankle.

"Parades can be reorganized," said Clementine. "And people will be talking about this for many years to come. The most important thing is that no one was harmed. And we've discovered that the hippogriff legend is actually true! I'd say today has been a success! Now, I'm going to leave you two to talk. Something tells me you need to sort some things out."

Harley looked over at Cosmo with red-rimmed eyes and saw his confused expression.

"I don't get it," he said. "The hippogriff machine was fine, but then it was like it suddenly woke from a sleep and had a mind of its own! It's a bit of a blur, but didn't you say something to it? Was that what triggered it? What in all clanking cogs were you thinking?"

"I was trying to catch your mum's attention and show everyone how amazing the robot hippogriff was – the first flying machine large enough to transport people without human control. I secretly added an electronic brain to Griffy so she can actually fly herself. And I wanted your mum to see you riding it, because it wasn't just about making an AI flying machine. I made the hippogriff as a gift for you, so you could have the best pet in Forgetown! I thought your mum would be so impressed she'd *have* to let you keep her, and then, when your mum wasn't paying attention, I activated the AI brain during the race because I thought Griffy would do something fancy to get her attention."

Cosmo's frown deepened. "You certainly did that."

Harley's heart clenched with the disappointment of failure.

"So that's why you were so controlling about making the hippogriff, and why you wouldn't listen to my ideas…"

"Yes, and I now know I should have listened. We could have worked as a team. If we had, maybe none of this calamity would have happened. Even the eel at the river thought I was hopeless."

Cosmo reached out and squeezed Harley's arm like she often did to him. "I actually think that's the kindest thing anyone has ever done for me."

"Really?"

"So it all went completely wrong." He shrugged. "I'm kind of used to the whirlwind of chaos that usually surrounds you." He laughed. "Although I do think my chances of getting a robot pet are slightly worse now."

"I'll make it right, I promise."

"I know you will. But do me a favour?"

"Anything."

"Let's work together on the solution this time."

She nodded, so hugely grateful to have the best friend in all of Inventia.

As if perfectly timed to knock Harley out of her moment of happiness, Fenelda Spiggot's voice suddenly called out, "Honestly, Harley!" She trudged towards them with a face like a thundercloud. "Just because you were going to lose the race didn't mean you had to go all extreme and cause the biggest

drama that Forgetown has ever seen! No one even saw me glide through the finishing hoop!" She slumped into the chair beside Harley.

Harley turned to Fenelda. "I'm sorry, Nel, really. I didn't mean to spoil it for you. You really did pull together an amazing flying machine."

Fenelda opened her mouth, shut it, then paused before saying, "Well, I'm just glad you're OK. You too, Cosmo."

"Who are you and what have you done to Nel?" Harley asked suspiciously.

"See, I can be unexpected too, Harley Hitch," Fenelda said with a smile.

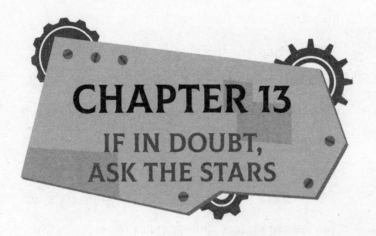

CHAPTER 13
IF IN DOUBT, ASK THE STARS

There was only one way to clear up a gigantic series of mishaps, and that was to make a colossal effort to put everything right. Harley needed to retrieve the hippogriff, repair its damaged wing, clear up the mess it had left behind, rearrange the parade, apologize to everyone and somehow find a way to make everything turn out the way it would have if it had all gone right in the first place.

Harley wrote it all in a list so she could tick things off.

"First stop, the hippogriffs. To get Griffy back."

Cosmo frowned. "But we've no idea where the hippogriffs took her. They've managed to keep themselves hidden for all these centuries. It won't be an easy task to find them."

"Ah, that's where my friends the stars come in! They have a perfect vantage point to see everything that happens. Plus, they're super nosy, so if anyone knows where the hippogriffs live, it'll be them."

"Good idea!"

Grandpa Elliot insisted they go first to Hitch House for some food and a change of clothes. They stopped off at Cosmo's house on the way, but his mum must have still been caught up dealing with the crowds back in town. He left a note to say he'd be at Harley's.

After dark, they hurried to the star-chatter observatory, where they found Professor Orbit, round glasses on, surrounded by star charts, working late … or, in his case, right on schedule.

He led them to the telescope. "You gave us all quite the scare earlier!"

"I'm sorry. I hope you're not too disappointed about the parade being cancelled. Clementine Brown thinks we can arrange it again soon."

"I'm used to it. Any number of things can ruin the skies – thunderclouds, hurricane winds, even a rogue robot hippogriff, it seems!" Professor Orbit swung the telescope into position. "There you are. I know Ursa Major is dying to speak to you."

"Harley, dahr-ling!" Ursa spun down in a glittering shimmer of light. She adjusted her tiara. "And I thought the stars were the only ones who could put on a good show! I tell you, Proxima and I were on the edge of our celestial seats watching the drama unfold!"

"How's the new opera coming along?" asked Harley.

"Wonderful, dahr-ling, simply sublime. The screech of your hippogriff actually inspired Alpha Centauri to write notes he'd never dreamed of before. Alpha! Proxima! Come down, Harley's here for a chat!"

"Harley, sweetie pops!" said Alpha, arriving in a shimmering gown and air-kissing her. "Are you all right? Any bruises? I can sprinkle stardust on you, if it helps."

Proxima appeared beside him, a dazzling star in his blue diamanté suit. "Harley! You're alive, thank the Universe! You had us terrified, simply sparkling with fear while we watched. And, Cosmo, you're alive too! I couldn't believe it when I saw that awful ironsting chasing you at the beginning of summer. It must have left quite the mark on your—"

"Enough of that, Proxima," said Ursa. "Harley clearly needs our help, and we are, as ever, at your twinkling service."

"I need to get Griffy back so I can mend her. Did you see where the hippogriffs took her?"

Alpha's hand shot up like a keen student's. Proxima's hand shot up too.

"They went to the eyrie," said Ursa.

Harley frowned. "Where's the eyrie? I've never heard of such a place."

"It's the name for their nest," said Alpha.

"OK … and where might I find this eyrie?"

"It's a long, long, long way from Forgetown. There's a single peak topped with snow beyond the Copper Mountains. But it'll take a mortal such as you months to walk there, or weeks on that trundle bike of your grandpa's."

"Weeks? But school starts again in a week, and I've got a parade to arrange and a million apologies to make, and—"

Cosmo tugged her sleeve. "And we're working as a team, remember? And this time *I* have a plan."

"You do?" said all the stars and Harley.

"Everything we need is on our doorstep," Cosmo said with a grin.

"We can't wait to see," said Proxima.

"Thanks. And I'll be back soon to speak to you about something else too," said Harley.

They said goodbye to the stars and Professor Orbit. Cosmo asked Grandpa Eden, who had been waiting outside, if they could visit Clementine Brown's flying castle.

"Sure thing. And you just missed your mum. She dashed past looking for you, then got caught up with a reporter from Inventia City. I told her you could stay with us as long as she needs to finish up and that we'd look after you tonight."

Cosmo gave a sad nod and Harley put a hand on his arm. "I'm sure she'll be able to catch up with you soon."

They hurried to the flying castle on the trundle bike.

"Shouldn't you two be tucked up in bed?"

Clementine asked when they arrived. "You've had quite the day."

"We're on our way home, but we wondered if you'd be free tomorrow?" said Cosmo. "We know the location of the hippogriffs, and we want to get the robot back. Except it's many weeks' travel from here on land, unless we could find a quicker way..."

Harley had guessed what Cosmo's idea was back at the star-chatter observatory, but she'd decided to take a back seat and let him explain and lead for once.

Clementine grinned. "Say no more. Meet me here at eight sharp in the morning and I'll have Razor ready."

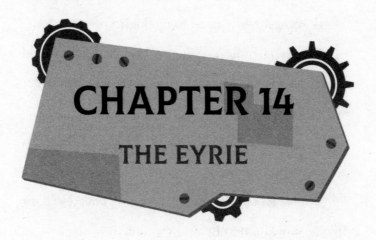

CHAPTER 14

THE EYRIE

The following morning Harley, Cosmo and Grandpa Eden met Clementine at the flying castle.

They climbed aboard, and the transporter lifted seamlessly into the sky. At the flick of a switch, they were bolting over the fields east of Forgetown.

"Did you try your mum again?" Harley asked Cosmo.

He nodded. "Yes, but her digi-com was busy *again*."

"I feel so terrible," said Harley. "I hope she gets a break soon. I really need to apologize properly too."

"Grandpa Elliot is going to help her today," said Grandpa Eden. "I'm sure you can catch her when we get back."

They tracked the course of the Rusty River up towards the Copper Mountains.

"Right, let's really make some progress! Hold on tight!" said Clementine.

Everything became a blur below as Clementine engaged the jet engines. They were pinned back with the thrust, and Harley and Cosmo laughed as their cheeks wobbled with the wind pressure. They raced over the hills, which quickly became the orangey Copper Mountains, the place where Harley had found the Moon hiding when it had gone missing earlier that year. Then they passed beyond the highest point of the range, and the mountains petered into a hilly valley. They zoomed through it to the other side where the landscape became flat apart from low plateaus of rock in the distance.

"There, look!" Harley said after a long while, pointing into the distance where an unmistakable pinnacle of rock, taller than the others, speared the landscape.

Clementine cut the booster jets and there was a lurch as Razor slowed. "The eyrie must be there. We'll make a gentle approach and circle round so we don't alarm the hippogriffs."

They spiralled up the pinnacle, slowly getting closer until Harley glimpsed what she thought was the nest at the top.

"There's nowhere to land. I can set the Razor close to the bottom, but you'll need to climb up."

It looked enormously steep, but the rocks were formed almost like a giant's winding staircase, so she felt confident they could make it, even if it took a while.

Clementine landed Razor, then Grandpa Eden

insisted on putting together a large lunch from the supplies he'd brought along.

"Are you sure you don't want us to come up too?" he asked.

Harley shook her head. "Cosmo and I will be fine. Too many of us might alarm the hippogriffs, and Clementine is the only one who can pilot the transport if we need a quick rescue. Sprocket can come, though. He's good at climbing, and it might help them understand about Griffy if they see another robot pet."

Clementine nodded. "That seems like a sensible plan."

Looking up made the climb seem impossibly long, but there was only one way to approach it: take the first step, then put one foot in front of the other.

"Off we go," said Harley, breathing in a bolstering lungful of air.

The structure of the mountain pinnacle meant natural rock steps spiralled round the edge in gradually decreasing width. Harley's leg muscles began burning quickly and they had to take lots of breaks. Sprocket bounded ahead with his springy, untiring legs and he kept coming back and yipping at them, impatient. After an hour they stopped for a rest and some food.

Harley looked out at the vast landscape of Inventia around them. There weren't any towns or villages in this area because it was quite dry beyond the Copper Mountains, but it had a rugged beauty. "The view from here is incredible. Look how far we've come!"

"Is that the Zinctile Plains in the far distance?" asked Cosmo.

"It could be. And look, there are Grandpa Eden and Clementine!" She pointed at two tiny dots beside the shimmering Razor far below and waved. She took her pocket telescope from her belt to see them more clearly. "They're chatting. I don't think they can see us this high up."

After they got their strength back, they continued onward. They barely spoke as they ascended, both needing to concentrate. The path was as wide as a transporter, but it still felt scary to be so high up and close to the edge; she didn't want to risk making a silly mistake and falling.

Eventually, the top was in sight, and as they turned the last corner, the hippogriffs came into view, gathered in an enormous twig-and-feather nest. Griffy was among them, looking out of place with her shining metal parts. The creatures turned to look at the children: ten sets of yellow, pin-sharp eyes studying them with suspicion. The air suddenly felt electric. Sprocket seemed unsure and hid behind

Cosmo's legs as Harley took a tentative step forward.

"Er, hello, hippogriffs," Harley said in what she hoped was a friendly voice. "I don't know how to speak hippogriff, but hopefully I can find some way to communicate with you all." She tried a smile, but they stared back distrustfully. "I'm grateful you came to Griffy's rescue, but she's not exactly like you. She's a robot pet. She'll need oiling and maintenance, and she can't stay here otherwise she'll seize up."

The ten hippogriffs tilted their heads, then the nearest one jumped up and began circling Harley. She tried not to look scared and tense, but her shoulders were almost by her ears. "Er, hi. It's nice to meet you." Harley gulped – it had a very sharp-looking beak.

Swift as a blink, it picked her up by the back of her belt and deposited her in the middle of the nest. It began slowly teasing her T-shirt with its beak.

"It's inspecting you! Perhaps it thinks you're their baby?" called Cosmo from the edge.

"Great," said Harley with a nervous giggle. The hippogriff stopped and sat down with the others, leaving her in the middle.

Harley stood up, brushed downy feathers from her clothes, and tried again. "OK, you don't understand human talk." She thought of the stars and decided to try acting. "Griffy there" – she pointed – "is a robot." She began simulating robotic movements with exaggerated style.

"What are you doing?" asked Cosmo with a bemused grin.

"Charades."

"That's meant to be a robot?"

Sprocket put his paws over his eyes.

"And if the robot ... isn't near tools" – she pointed to her belt – "then she will rust." Harley carried on

dancing like a dramatic robot in the middle of the nest, then began slowing down to signify gradually freezing, before finally becoming motionless. She held the pose for ten long seconds while the hippogriffs stared at her, perplexed.

"Good effort, Harley!" Cosmo called, trying to contain a giggle. "But I don't think they understand."

Cosmo stepped forward. He cleared his throat, then he began a series of screeches and whistles.

"Er, what are you doing?" asked Harley, bewildered.

The hippogriffs studied him with intent yellow eyes, then shared a look between themselves and gave a nod. Whatever Cosmo had just done seemed to connect with them.

"Lucky for you, I read a brilliant book about bird calls while you were ignoring me earlier this summer. There are some great audiobooks in the library too. I learned a bit of eagle, which might work?"

"Oh, so *that's* what all that strange whistling you were doing back in Forgetown was! Why didn't you say when we got here?"

"It was too much fun watching you robot dance!" He gave another series of screeches.

"What did you say?" asked Harley.

"I explained about Griffy and asked if we may please take her back now."

The hippogriff who had picked Harley up whistle-screeched back to Cosmo.

Harley looked at it, then Cosmo eyes wide. "What did it say?"

Cosmo frowned so deeply his glasses slid down his nose. "They're going to eat us."

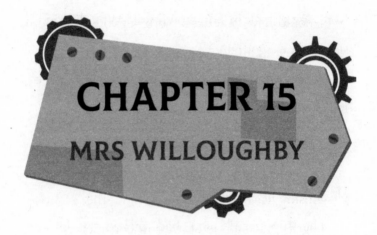

CHAPTER 15
MRS WILLOUGHBY

"What?!" Harley exclaimed as her heart raced.

Cosmo's frown softened. "Ah, I get it, sorry, not *eat us*; they're going to *let us*! The whistle for the two words is very similar."

"Don't scare me like that!"

The hippogriff whistled something at Griffy, who gave a nod. Then Griffy walked towards Harley, who stroked the silvery feathers of her neck.

"Sorry about what happened back in Forgetown. We should have practised more, let you get used to everything. Shall we go home and try again?"

Griffy dipped her beak and Harley led her to the edge of the nest beside Cosmo.

"How do I say thank you in hippogriff?" Harley asked.

Cosmo gave a low whistle and the group of hippogriffs gave a nod of acknowledgement.

Harley led the robot hippogriff out of the eyrie alongside Cosmo, and she turned to him. "Have I told you lately that you're brilliant?"

Cosmo grinned. "So are you. We make a good team."

Harley patted Griffy. "Come on, let's get you home."

Suddenly they heard a high-pitched sound.

Harley frowned. "Was that another hippogriff?"

Cosmo shook his head. "Nope. I recognize that tone – it sounds like my mum calling for me!"

Harley looked over to see Fenelda's flying machine hovering next to the mountain, with Mrs Willoughby in the driving seat!

"Mum!" Cosmo yelled.

"Cosmo!"

"What are you doing?"

"That nice Fenelda Spiggot lent this to me. I've been trying to get to you since yesterday. I kept getting waylaid by duties, but I decided I'd had enough and had to tell you straight away!" said Mrs Willoughby.

"You could have waited for us to get back!"

She shook her head. "I wanted to tell you immediately!"

"We'll meet you at the bottom of the mountain. Grandpa Eden and Clementine are down there!"

"No, I have to tell you now!"

"Mum, are you sure you're all right?" Cosmo asked doubtfully.

Mrs Willoughby's cheeks were glowing and her eyes sparkled. "Yes. It came to me in a blast this morning. I realized how much effort Harley had gone to for your happiness and how her intentions, although a little unfortunate, were truly caring. It made me see my own failings, how I've been so wrapped up with work that I've not spent a single day of the summer with you! I feel positively dreadful."

"But I understand that your job is important. It's honestly all right, Mum."

"It's not all right. I knew you wanted a robot pet, ever since that first day at Cogworks. Yet I refused to have the conversation with you. I should have made time. The truth is, I just find it hard to let go of the controls at work sometimes."

Cosmo glanced at Harley. "I know someone else a bit like that."

"Can you forgive me, Cosmo?"

"Of course I can!"

They both smiled.

"I'm really, really, really sorry about what happened, Mrs Willoughby!" called Harley.

"It's all right. It helped me come to my senses. In fact, I've taken the rest of the school holiday off," Mrs Willoughby said. "Cosmo, we can do anything you like!"

"I do have an idea for one thing we could do together. Meet me at the bottom!"

Mrs Willoughby nodded and flew down.

"Oh, I nearly forgot." Cosmo dashed back to the nest and whistle-spoke to the hippogriffs.

"What did you ask them?" said Harley.

"You'll soon find out," he said, winking.

It was faster getting down the pinnacle, even though they had to lead Griffy.

"All sorted, I see!" said Grandpa Eden at the bottom.

"I don't want to risk flying Griffy back until we've fixed her wing," said Harley.

Clementine smiled. "There's plenty of room in the Razor. She can go in the back and the rest of us can squeeze in. I'll tow Miss Spiggot's machine, and Mrs Willoughby can join us for the journey home."

"I can't wait!" said Mrs Willoughby.

"Mum, I thought you might come and help me and Harley mend Griffy," said Cosmo.

Mrs Willoughby gave him a hug. "I'd love to."

The next day, Harley, Cosmo and Mrs Willoughby set to work on repairing the hippogriff in the garage of Hitch House. It turned out that Mrs Willoughby was excellent at robotics, having studied it at Inventia City University, and she explained lots of interesting details about programming circuits while the grandpas brought in snacks and drinks.

At one point, Harley left Cosmo and his mum to work on their own, taking some time with Sprocket outside. "I haven't had much time for you this summer either. How about we play fetch?"

Sprocket's eyes filled with flashing hearts.

That evening, Griffy flew her test runs perfectly.

While Mrs Willoughby was chatting to Grandpa Eden, Harley gave Cosmo a nudge. "I think it's time to ask her about the pet."

Cosmo smiled as they walked over. "Mum, I was thinking about the robot pet. I like Griffy a lot, but she's not the most practical pet, and her best skill is flying. I was thinking, if Harley doesn't mind, that maybe *you* could look after her as *your* pet. You often have to dash off to Inventia for meetings, and Griffy would get you there twice as fast, which would mean more free time for us to spend together."

"What a thoughtful idea." Mrs Willoughby smiled. "But I do think it's time you had your own pet too."

Harley stepped forward. "I have an idea. With your permission, that is." She whispered in Mrs Willoughby's ear, then they exchanged a smile.

"Perfect."

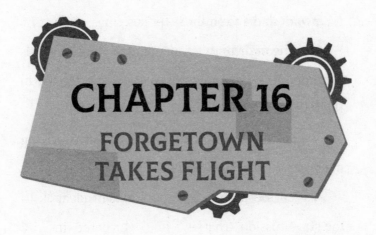

CHAPTER 16
FORGETOWN TAKES FLIGHT

The Aviation Parade was rearranged for the second-to-last day of the holidays. True to her word, Mrs Willoughby took the time off and left it to her capable team to handle the organization. Cosmo, however, was busy running around. When Harley saw him whispering to Clementine, she knew something was going on.

"What are you up to?"

But he would only reply: "There's a time for teamwork and a time for surprises…"

On the morning of the parade, huge crowds streamed into Forgetown once more. Cosmo sat in the VIP area with his mum and Harley.

"I can't wait to finally see the visiting flying machines in action!" said Harley.

A great horn sounded and Clementine took to the stage.

"People of Inventia! After an unexpected delay, the Aviation Parade is proud to come to you this year from Forgetown, with its extraordinary people and even better ice cream!"

The crowd cheered.

"Sit back, relax and enjoy the show, and don't leave early. You don't want to miss a special surprise…"

An *ooh* of expectation sounded from the crowds.

Then, from somewhere behind the Iron Forest, the first flying machine of the parade rose into the sky: a spectacular airship shaped like a swan. It glided past the audience.

A more traditional hot-air balloon took to the skies behind it, but as it got nearer it became clear that underneath was a great galleon.

More flying vehicles followed, each more spectacular and captivating than the last: an airship with tendrils trailing behind it so the whole thing looked like a gravity-defying octopus; a fleet of aviators with dragon wings and thrusters who flew in formation, leaving trails of coloured gas in the sky; multi-ballooned sky boats with tightropes between them for aviators to walk along, balancing with umbrellas; and an airship shaped like a whale with parachutists jumping from it and dancing before the crowds.

It was spectacular, and the crowds cheered, clapped and stared in awe as the sky filled with vehicles moving in a slow parade across the skies above Forgetown.

At the end, Clementine Brown took to the sky in Razor, flying above all the other marvels. Her jets powered with air-popping speed and she zoomed across the sky like lightning, shaving half a second off her own record. The crowd erupted in cheers.

Gradually all the flying machines landed in the fields opposite Rusty River, and Clementine took to the stage again. "For the first time in the history of the Aviation Parade, we would now like to invite the audience to take part."

The crowd fell silent, people looking at one another with questioning looks.

Then a stream of small hot-air balloons with miniature baskets flew out of the castle. The aviators with dragon wings flew out with passenger harnesses and landed before the crowd, inviting the audience to step forward and take to the skies with them.

Harley looked to Cosmo, who smiled knowingly. "This was your idea, wasn't it?"

Cosmo grinned, then cupped his hand and screeched.

Ten hippogriffs rose from behind the old mill and flew to him. "They agreed to come back and give some rides!" Cosmo said, grinning.

"So *that's* what you asked them back at the eyrie!" Bubbles of excitement made Harley feel like she could burst. Riding a real hippogriff would be the thrill of a lifetime!

Harley and Cosmo chose a hippogriff each and jumped on to their backs.

"Ready?" called Cosmo.

With a couple of strong beats, the hippogriffs took flight. The wind rushed through Harley's pink hair as they soared elegantly above Forgetown.

Soon small balloons filled the sky as hundreds of visitors took to the air.

Harley had to admit that it was nice to take a back seat with the ideas for a change and see Cosmo take the lead. Sometimes all she needed was to listen to her friends and the best ideas would fly.

They raced over the Iron Forest and circled the dome of Cogworks school. All around was laughter, smiles and whoops of joy. Taking flight together lifted everyone.

Later, as the sun set, Sprocket activated his disco lights – a new addition – and everyone danced into the evening. Harley had asked the stars to come down, and Ursa, Alpha and Proxima sang a special opera called *Flight* for everyone.

During the performance, Fenelda sidled up to Harley. She unclipped the golden light-bulb pin from her T-shirt, the Pupil of the Term prize she was sharing with Harley, and passed it to her with an eye roll.

"Fair's fair. I reckon you mended things pretty well, so it's your turn to wear this."

"Nel, if you keep on being nice, I might have to call you a friend." Harley grinned.

"Steady on, Hitch. I'm planning on beating you in every assignment and winning it all back next term." Fenelda flicked her perfect bobbed hair and walked breezily away, but Harley saw the hint of a smile on her lips, and not a mean one. A smile that said there *was* a friendship – in whatever strange form it might be – between them.

Grandpas Elliot and Eden found Harley. "We popped home and there was a package on the doorstep for you."

She clenched her hands in excitement. "Brilliant!"

The aviation extravaganza eventually drew to a happy close as people made their way home and the aviators began to pack away their machines.

Harley went to say goodbye to Clementine. "Thank you so much for coming to Forgetown."

Clementine beamed at her. "Our pleasure. It's been our favourite parade ever. Your hippogriff innovation really is groundbreaking. It seems to me there's a lot of potential to explore in combining AI with transport. Of course, it comes with risks to manage, and I know you see that, but the world needs people like you, Harley. And I meant it about the job, you know. When you've finished your schooling, there will always be a position for you with us. Maybe we can invent the next great flying machine and make that dream of going to space a reality for you."

Harley filled her lungs with a satisfying gulp of air and looked up at the twinkling stars. "I'd really like that."

Clementine took off her aviator goggles and put

them on Harley's head. "Well, until then, you can keep these."

Harley's heart swelled.

The following afternoon, Harley knocked on Cosmo's front door holding a large box tied with a big red bow.

"For you!" Harley said, thrusting it into his arms. She'd already opened it and made a few of her own adjustments that morning, before carefully repackaging it.

"What is it?"

"An empty box."

"Really?"

"Of course not! Just open it!"

Cosmo undid the ribbon, ripped the paper away and opened the box. His mouth fell open. "Harley, it's amazing. How did you…? Where did you…? I mean, did Mum…?"

Harley grinned, barely able to contain her excitement. "Yes, we have her permission. What do you think?"

He reached both arms inside and pulled out a beautiful silver robot owl.

"I thought it would be a bit more manageable than the hippogriff, and I tried to think of something that suited you, rather than going for the most impressive thing I could think of, and you love books and nature, and owls symbolize wisdom, and I think you're always pretty wise—"

"Harley, stop talking. She's utterly perfect."

"Well, she was, but I simply had to add some fancy adjustments. Remember those light bulbs we found at the beginning of the holidays which I used for Sprocket? Well, your owl is *also* the proud owner of a disco setting, and there's a muffin compartment too, *and* her beak now glows in the dark!"

"Great!" He beamed with a smile big enough to light up Forgetown.

"Now, I must dash," said Harley. "School starts tomorrow and I need to change my hair. Do you want to know what colour I'm going for next?"

"I think I'll let you surprise me, like always."

She gave him a big grin, then, with Sprocket at her heels, she danced down the path like a brilliant firework of chaos.

ACKNOWLEDGEMENTS

My hippogriff-sized thanks to the Scholastic UK team – Linas Alsenas, Julia Sanderson, Lauren Fortune, Kate Shaw, George Ermos, Jamie Gregory, Sarah Dutton, Wendy Shakespeare, Olivia Towers, Kiran Khanom – and all the booksellers, educators and librarians who continue to support my stories and work so hard to inspire young readers.

Vashti Hardy grew up in West Sussex between the hills and the sea, scrambling through brambles and over pebbles. Her middle-grade fantasy novels are now published across the world in several languages. Her debut, *Brightstorm*, was shortlisted for the Waterstones Children's Book Prize and Books Are My Bag Readers Awards, and her second book, *Wildspark*, won the Blue Peter Book Award 'Best Story' in 2020. Vashti now lives in both West Sussex and Lancashire with her husband and three children.

Vashtihardy.com
Twitter @vashti_hardy
Instagram vashtihardyauthor

George Ermos is an illustrator, maker and avid reader from England. He works digitally and loves illustrating all things curious and mysterious. He is always trying to incorporate new artiness from the various world cultures he reads about and explores.

Twitter @georgermos

READ MORE OF
HARLEY'S ADVENTURES: